S.P. SOMTOW

MIRIAM

MEMOIRS OF A GODDESS

PART ONE
ANNUNCIATION

Miriam: Memoirs of a Goddess
One: Annunciation

A BRIEF APOLOGIA

You are about to read a work of fiction. No one is claiming that anything described herein really happened. Although inspired by events that many people consider to be historical, the happenings in this book have their basis only in one writer's imagination.

Nonetheless, a brief explanation might be in order.

On a bleak day in 1997, a humdrum day in suburban Los Angeles, I was lying on the couch, profoundly depressed by the direction my career was going. I had written over thirty books in all sorts of milieux, but now I seemed to have reached an impasse.

Lying on my stomach as a current issue of *Time* magazine in which there was an article about how the Pope was considering making the Virgin Mary Co-Redemptrix — an honour not unlike when the ancient Roman

Senate used to elevate dead emperors to godhood.

For some strange reason, I fell into a kind of reverie — a kind of dream-meditation about the Virgin Mary. Perhaps it was because so much has been said of her lately, so many visions of her in all her splendor have been seen by so many people amid apocalyptic and millennial fervor.

Suddenly, in the midst of this reverie, I heard a woman's voice cry out: "But what about *me?*" Startled, I opened my eyes to catch a fleeting glimpse of a woman as my dream faded. She was no goddess. She was an ordinary woman, flawed and very much human, and she was telling me that she, too, had a story to tell.

I realized then that we are in danger of forgetting, so awed are we by the spectacle of divine grace, so enraptured are we by this image of perfect motherhood and godliness, that within this radiant and mythic archetype of the Queen of Heaven there is also a human being.

This novel is not written to diminish the power of faith, nor is it written to denigrate the truthfulness of religion. It should certainly not be viewed as an attack on any-one's beliefs.   The truth that underlies all the world's great myths would not be truth were it not firmly anchored to our common humanity.

But I want to insist there is no magic here.   No disappearing tablets, no angelic visitations. *I made this novel up.* Let me be right up front about that.   I have tried to adhere to those few scraps which impartial scholars generally agree to be facts, and to recreate as plausibly as I can the world and world-view of Rome in the 1st Century.   As for the rest, it is all imagination; and if my readers find themselves too angered by that, then please remember that it is only fiction.

MIRIAM

MEMOIRS OF A GODDESS

I
Annunciation

1

It was an ugly house, small and unswept, dusty and dark. I was an ugly woman, old before my time, disheveled and disconnected from the world. I was a bitter woman who entertained neither guests nor kinfolk, let alone angels.

Yet, one day, one cold, unpleasant day, one bleak day in an interminable succession of cold bleak days, there came to me a certain man....

"I have to talk to you," he said, "about your son."

I looked at this man, who had barged in without getting anyone to announce him, who had found me leavening dough on a bench in the atrium. He was sitting at my feet now, looking up at me. His beard was trimmed, his clothing Roman, and he spoke

Greek to me, but he couldn't hide his ethnic origins; I went on kneading my dough, and answered him in Aramaic; when I try to speak Greek it sticks in my craw. He was hardly what one might call an angel.

"Are you from the secret police?" I asked him.

"I used to be," he said. "It's true, then, what they say ... that you see right into the soul of a man."

He kissed my callused feet.

"What are you selling?" I asked him.

"Selling? What can I possibly sell you, mother to the world, queen of the earth and sky?"

I started to smile. Then I reflected. He was one of those people who are always trying to disarm you. Such people are dangerous. They look at you with such earnestness, such openness, that you forget yourself with them; and I never want to forget myself again.

"Didn't your son once compare the kingdom of heaven to a woman leavening dough?" he said. "It's good when the metaphors match up so perfectly; less work for the bringer of tidings."

"So what," I said, "has he done this time? People always think he's trying to start a revolution, but you know he's not the type; he just wants a little more purity of heart, a little closer observation of the spirit of the Torah; I never understood why that should get a man in trouble."

"You speak of him in the present tense?" the man said.

"Why, have you arrested him? Have you tortured him? Is he dead?"

"No." He laughed, a dry, throat-clearing sort of laugh. I know I was not the woman he expected to find here, and he was trying to adjust himself, chart a quick new course; looking at him, I decided he was not dangerous after all. I tossed the dough in a basket and covered it with a cloth.

"He might be better off behind bars," I said. "I haven't seen him for a month or more, and when I do see him it's always: James, don't antagonize the Romans; James, don't irritate the Sanhedrin; James, don't dine in public with the Zealots."

The man laughed again, but this time it was hearty, melodious. "I haven't come here to talk about *him*. I want to talk about your other son. You know ... the one that...."

"Get out of my house," I said.

"But you haven't heard my proposition —
"

"Get out of my house. And don't bother to tell me your name. I don't want to see you again."

"It's Saul, I mean Paul."

***

In the morning, he ambushed me by the well. I fetch my own water; I don't live the way I used to, when we still had money. That day, I regretted it when I set the jar down to await my turn; for I saw him, sitting on a bench beneath a battered stucco Nike, scribbling on a wax tablet. I fetch my water very early; I've reached the age when one sleeps very little. He must have been there since before dawn.

"Miriam," he said, "at least let me tell you why I've come."

I walked away from him, but I did not want to create a scene; under the archway, a legionary stood guard, and you never know how they are going to react. Being universally hated, they panic easily. Of course, we wouldn't have fresh water without them, with all their aqueducts and water-works, but people do tend to forget that.

"I've ridden a long way. All the way from Damascus. Miriam, I've seen your son."

"Everyone seems to have seen him except me," I said. I drew my water and filled the stoneware amphora. I lifted it up. I was about to balance it on my head when he grasped the handles, wrenched away the jar.

"At least," he said, "let me be your water-bearer. We can't have someone of your stature carrying your own water."

He did not put it on his head or his shoulder; instead, he cradled the jar in both arms. He was not used to this sort of thing. "Forgive me," he said, when at last, for the first time, he managed to elicit a smile from me.

"You shouldn't try to do a woman's work," I said. But not wanting him to lose face, I let him struggle with the water-jar, all the way down the alley, until he reached my front gate; then, with no one to see, I took the jar from him, hefted it up, and carried it inside.

"I would have carried it, Miriam," he

gasped. "I mean, your frailty, your advanced years —"

"Sometimes I feel I've borne the world on my shoulders," I said, "and not just a jug of water."

"Oh, Miriam," said this Paul, or Saul, "you have, you surely have."

"I suppose," I said, "now that you've carried this jar of water for me — a thing I could much easier have done myself — you will now say I am obliged to share with you the bread I baked yesterday."

"You do me an honor far beyond what I deserve."

What a tongue he had! No need for dessert this morning, I could see. "I think we even have some salt left," I said, "and an unopened cask of Chian wine; you see, civilization *has* reached these parts."

"*Eukharistô.*"

"No, Paul," I said, "speak Aramaic. You're a Jew; act like one. Too much Greek can give you ulcers."

"I'm sorry, mother." He made the switch very smoothly.

I called the slave — I only have one, a wretched Samaritan named Jonathan —

and we had breakfast in the triclinium —
yes, on real Roman couches, even though
they were shabby, patched in a couple of
places. All the furniture I had was hand-
me-downs from my family friend's mansion
in Arimathea.

We broke bread. We reclined. We had a
modest amount of wine, watered four parts
to one; and at last my visitor allowed himself to utter the name I had tried to forget.
"It's your other son I've come about, Miriam.
Don't pretend you never think about Joshua
bar Joseph."

Yes, he had said it. And all unbidden, I
began to weep. "I'm sorry," I said. "You
weren't there. You don't know."

"But I do," he said, and reached across the
tabletop to hold my hand, and looked at me
with those eyes, luminous with love and
demonic with ferocity. His was a soft hand;
no physical labor in *his* background.
"Mother, I've seen your son."

So that was all this was about. "Another
sighting," I said. I shrugged. "Some people
will never learn."

Crucifixions are common, but you never
get used to them. My son's was more merci-

ful than most — it only lasted three hours. Yet ... the man did not understand how cruel it was to remind me, to torment me with yet another bogus apparition.

"More than a sighting," said Paul. "I had a vision so powerful it threw me from my horse and afflicted me with temporary blindness. It's an idea so grand, so all-encompassing that it will change the entire world."

I had heard that many times before. It was the cant of the traveling salesman. A new kind of lantern, a brighter-burning oil, a new technique for the latchwork of rugs that won't retain dust, a tastier breed of chicken; the Romans, who are so anxious to sell their brand of civilization, are the worst of the lot, though they of all people can claim most honestly that they *have* changed the world.

"All right," I said. "Tell me of your vision, since you won't go away until you have."

"I want to start a new religion."

This time I really laughed. Heartily. The idea of this intense little man playing Moses was beyond belief. "You!" I said. "Oh, have some more wine."

But he didn't laugh, didn't even smile; he was quite, quite serious. "Mother," he said, "inside the tawdry biography of Joshua bar Joseph there is a profound truth waiting to be revealed. It is, perhaps, the greatest truth since Moses penned the Pentateuch. There is a story inside your son's story that is the story of all great mythic heroes, of gods who descend to earth, are made flesh, redeem the world, sacrifice their mortal lives to become the life-blood of the world, and are reborn in glory to ascend to the bosom of the sun — of Dionysus, Horus, Adonais, and Osiris. This is bigger than a failed revolution in a barbaric outpost at the edge of the world. This is a grand idea that will raze the foundations of the Empire. I'm going to sell your son to the Gentiles, Miriam."

"It's been done, Paul," I said bitterly. "I believe the going rate was thirty shekels."

"His body may have been worth thirty denarii," said Paul, "but his soul will be worth more than the whole world."

"And what do you know of his soul?" I said. "You never even knew him."

"Listen to me," he said. "Do you know

what truth is?"

"Of course," I said.   "Everyone knows that."

"It's strange that you should say that," he said, "because if everyone really knew that, why would there be this desperate search for truth, why would our philosophers, our rabbis, our magicians, our common folk be so obsessed with the need to find it? It's not truth that everyone knows, Miriam; it's reality."

"And what is the difference?" I asked him, thinking that he would launch into one of those fashionable philosophical arguments that are so popular in the wineshops of the young.

"Reality," said Paul, "is what you touch and feel. It's this loaf of bread, this jug of wine." He flicked it with a finger. "It's the pain you feel when you bump into a wall. It's the heat and the cold, it's the things you do and see and touch. Behind reality," he went on, staring at me with an intensity one usually sees in priests or madmen, "is truth. You can't touch truth. Truth is what reality means. It tells us why we're here. It tells us what we are."

"So what is the truth inside you, then?"

"In reality, a messenger; in truth, an angel," he said, switching to Greek to make some strained word-play out of our word for angel and their word for messenger.

"And what, then, was my son?"

"In reality," said Paul, "just another failed messiah. A misguided idealist. Too good for this world, really. Used by politicians, worshipped for all the wrong reasons; in the wrong place at the wrong time; a victim. But in truth, mother, in truth ... the light of the world."

"Then go your way, Paul or Saul. Your Joshua is not the Joshua I knew. I'm not intelligent enough to distinguish your reality from your truth; to me it's all talk. It sounds wonderful, your new religion; may you do as well as the Isis-priests and the Mithraists and the women who guard the Mysteries of Eleusis; but I'm perfectly happy to remain sitting here, drawing my small pension from Joseph of Arimathea's secretary, baking my bread and scolding my surviving children."

"I need you."

"If you want me to endorse your religion, I suppose I shall; I know your sort pretty well, I've raised sons, been a rabbi's wife and a rabbi's mother; even if I don't, you'll only say that I did, and argue it in such a way that I can't quite deny it."

"Endorsing won't be enough."

At that point, I was ready to throw this man out of my house a second time. This was dangerous man, if only because he had perfected the art of wearing someone down. He was a total stranger, not even a kinsman's kinsman; he had been rude; he was trying to subvert my mind with ideas that, if not downright blasphemous, were at the very least unorthodox. And I didn't like him. I suppose I should have had my slave show him the door right then and there, but curiosity prompted me to ask him a final question. "And so, Paul, messenger or angel, what is *my* truth? Do you not see an ugly woman, old before her time, in an ugly unswept house far from the city, a bitter woman who never receives guests, a woman who has been losing her children one by one to madness and execution? What truth will come from this miserable excuse for reality? What will you and this cosmic new religion make of me?"

He said, "I'm going to make you the mother of God."

2

When I was pregnant and thirteen, I had never heard of Bethlehem.   I had never heard of much; good girls are not supposed to know anything.   Bethlehem was a midrash, which is to say that, because certain prophets and certain great experts on those prophets had agreed that the kvisatz haderach was to be born in Bethlehem, reality had perforce to be edited a little, in the name of truth.

Being pregnant, thirteen, and unmarried, I abruptly lost the designation of *good girl*. I was therefore no longer required to be ignorant; my world, consequently, became much larger, much more exhilarating, and much more terrifying.

As I listened to Paul's astonishing revelations about a life I never, in the flesh, lived, I realized that I had heard that phrase before ... in the same unschooled Greek that is the lingua franca of the Empire ... *mēter tou theoû*. But it hadn't meant quite the same thing, because the person who uttered this phrase to me had no particular god in mind. He meant to say, "Miriam, Miriam, you could even be mother to a god."

He was a centurion who had been billeted in my father's house, and his name was Pantera.

***

Our house in Nazareth was neither small nor ugly, which is why, I suppose, it attracted the attention of the garrison commander. It was a Roman-style house, its rooms opening into a central atrium. No statues, of course, and the fountain had an abstract floral motif — but it was a house that foreigners might condescendingly deem civilized — indeed, the only such house in Nazareth, though there were many such in Sepphoris, of course, a hour's walk away.

My father did not descend from kings —

the only king in Galilee was Herod, called the Great, and he ruled only on imperial suffrance — but he was wealthy enough to make me a desirable match. I was to marry Joseph, a scholar so skilled at constructing interpretations of the Torah that his friends nicknamed him the Carpenter. I had seen him a few times, always in the company of cousins, brothers, and other guardians of propriety; he seemed decent enough, in a diffident sort of way; it wasn't, of course my business to know too much about my future husband; that was an affair for my elders. If Nazareth wasn't such a small town, I might not even have seen him before the wedding.

We were a just little bit Greek in our habits — not shockingly so, but just enough to be modern, and to scandalize the neighbors — my father regularly went to Alexandria on business, and brought back souvenirs: a terracotta Harpocrates, a bust of Alexander, and once a scroll of Sappho, whose poetry, he told us, was not unlike the *Song of Songs*. As I say, we were modern. We actually had the odd graven image around the house, and frequently had foreigners to dinner, Romans even.

Not that I attended any dinners; I waited out such affairs in the women's wing of the house, along with my slave, who had once been my wet-nurse, the vastly rotund Ruth, whose name in the original Anatolian tongue was unpronounceable.

My doll's name was Shoshana. She came from Alexandria. I cradled her, rocked her back and forth; this evening, though, I saw quite clearly that one terracotta arm was broken off, and one lapis eye was missing. I put her away in my treasure chest, and I said, "I'll never play with dolls again. They're graven images, anyway; none of my cousins has one."

"*He's* here tonight, you know," Ruth said, as she finished combing my hair.

"You mean my future husband?" I said.

"No, no," she said, "well of course he's here too, but I mean the centurion. Such a man! So gnarled, so scarred, so gloomy! But he sings to you with his eyes. You have to look at him, you know. I'll take you; we'll pretend to be raiding the larder."

"Shouldn't I really be —"

"Yes, yes. I'll take the blame for it, I suppose, little mistress."   She knew I how yearned for the slightest glimpse of the outside world. I'd been afflicted by a strange lightheadedness all morning, thought I might be coming down with a fever; but I let Ruth pull me from the women's quarters. "Come on, dear. You've been unconscionably irritable for days; time to look at something new, even if it's only a man."

She took my hand and propelled me down the corridor; it was a secret corridor which allowed the women to sequester themselves at a moment's notice, if a strange man came calling; we did not use it much, for few strange men ever did come calling; instead it was crammed with cracked amphorae, unmended furniture, a battered olive press, and other things my mother could not bear to throw away. Oh yes, a broken loom. It was easy for me to squeeze my way past all the rubbish; but I had to move the loom to let Ruth waddle through. Presently we reached the larder; one door opened into the kitchen, another, open a crack, afforded a view of the triclinium. As always, the tiny room reeked of cedarwood and olives. I stuck my nose in the crack in the door, peered out.

My future husband and my father were deep in conversation. They were comparing messiahs, which was then as now a favorite sport.

"It's the taxes," my father said. "Before the Romans came, every seventh year was tax-free — now we have double taxation, the imperial tax and the taxes of Herod. Whenever people feel oppressed, you get a plague of messiahs."

"The most successful messiahs are the ones who offer hope, not promises," said Joseph. "Hope keeps men alive; promises can't be kept. You can't get rid of the Romans; you might as well try to get rid of the noonday sun; you may hate how it saps your strength, but you have to live with it."

"What about divine intervention?" said my father.

"I'm afraid that the Lord God of Abraham, Isaac and Jacob probably feels rather abandoned these days. Plenty of decadence everywhere. Didn't I see you at the theater in Sepphoris last month? Euripides, wasn't it?"

"Quite so," said my father, "and when you have business dealings with the outside world, you can't always ignore what passes for culture among the heathen. Besides ... how do you know I was there, if you weren't there yourself?"

"My point exactly, father ... none of us deserves a kvisatz haderach. We all dream of such, but I'm a practical man, too; I'm logical; that's why they call me the Carpenter."

"But then again, Carpenter, gods are not logical — not even yours."   Both men looked up. It was the centurion who spoke. He was not old, but his face was pitted with scars, and there was one in particular, a thin white line that crossed from left cheek to right brow, like a crack in a jar; but his voice was deep, and the Greek he spoke drenched with an unfamiliar music. His cuirass was as mottled as his face. His helmet, I now saw, lay on a low tiled table next to a plate of figs.   I ducked behind an amphora, but I think he saw me. Perhaps it was Ruth's giggling that made him look. I think our eyes met. I was too well brought up to have remembered the moment too clearly. I think he smiled.

"The Lord of Hosts is a lot more logical than some of your strange specimens," said the Carpenter. "Fornicating in the guise of bulls and golden showers, squabbling like fishwives — not much dignity there."

The centurion laughed a little. He did not, I think, mean to offend; he simply did not know how things are in Galilee. "But," he said, "you must admit there is one failure of logic — you claim that your god is the most powerful force in the universe, yet it is those fornicating bulls who rule the world."

This was a rather tactless thing to say, and I could see my father start to fulminate, only he couldn't, not in front of the Roman military — seeing he'd gone too far, Pantera hastened to add, "I don't hold with all those rutting animal gods myself, you understand; I'm a disciple of the Magna Mater."

"Oh, little mistress," Ruth whispered, "he has the true religion." For Ruth, of course, was an idolater.

I stared at the man. I was getting dizzy for some reason. This time I am sure he saw me. I am sure his eyes met mine, because I was struck by their color: a deep blue-gray, like the Sea of Galilee. Young clear eyes, set amid battered features.

Suddenly my dizziness grew into a kind

of woozy bewilderment — I swayed, I
clutched the handle of the door only to find
myself pushing it open, and before I could
stop myself —

Ruth screamed.   I let go the door and
found myself reaching out for the first sup-
port I could — which happened to be the
shoulders of the centurion.   My hands
gripped leather and brass.   He smelled of
cloves, of sweat, of blood and dust.   The
centurion laughed — he was the only person who seemed unaware of the impropri-
ety of it all — and then something even
worse happened.

Something was oozing out of me. A dark
stain seeping through my undertunic to
redden my costly, snowy-white Greek chi-
ton. I knew what it was — I had been told
it would happen one day — but why now? I
let go of the stranger. Shame flushed my
face. Joseph and my father backed away.
Ruth began shouting for my mother, who
marched in grimly from the other side of
the house, through the atrium.

"What's happening to me?" I said.   I
could see shame on the men's faces ... all except the centurion's. He sympathized with

me.

"Don't be afraid, girl," he said. "I have a little sister back in Ephesus, and I know what you're going through. Such a pretty girl!" He reached his arm out, tenderly, meaning to caress my cheek or otherwise comfort me, I'm sure; but at that moment my mother stormed up to us and slapped the centurion out of the way. "You fool!" she said. "You'll have to be purified now. My daughter is *niddah* — menstruating, unclean."

A searing cramp racked my lower body. I whimpered. Why hadn't anyone told me it would come upon me so suddenly? I'd heard the village girls make jokes about it, of course. I hadn't realized it would hurt. I hadn't realized it would smell.

"Don't touch *any* of the men — especially Joseph! — do you understand, Miriam? If you touch a man, he will be unclean till evening; and you don't want to inconvenience your father in any way. You'll have to stay in your room for seven days; Ruth will take your meals to you; after that we'll have a mikvah."

"Really, mistress," said the centurion, "I

was only trying to soothe her; understandably, she's upset, if this has never happened before —"

"You are our guest, centurion" my mother said, "even if we didn't exactly invite you; I won't have you polluted. Ruth, take her away. Oh, oh, what a time for this to happen! My husband, you must beat her."

"How can I possibly beat her? She's unclean. All right, all right then, after her mikvah." I knew that my father would somehow contrive to forget. He loved me well, for all that he was sometimes remote, or too absorbed in his bookkeeping.

"Well," said my mother, "at least beat that miserable slave for sneaking her into the larder to gawk at our visitors."

Quickly, Ruth hustled me down the corridor. Beating the servants is a necessary evil, as is beating one's daughter — *for he who spareth the rod loveth not his child* — but in my father's house it was more often threat than a reality. Still, my mother seemed more agitated than usual.

"I didn't do anything!" I sobbed, and Ruth comforted me, murmuring over and over, "Yes, little mistress, yes little mistress."

My mother, taking the long way round, now met me in front of my room with an armful of wet rags. "You'd better do a thorough job of cleansing her off," she said. She barely looked at me as the slave opened the door to my chamber.

Ruth's countenance was dour when my mother was looking, but as soon as she closed the door she broke out in a gap-toothed grin. She embrace me heartily, without any sense of repugnance, and, after making sure my mother's footsteps had died down the corridor, cried, "Praise to the Mother! My little mistress has become a woman!"

3

Ruth held me in her arms that night, and sang to me some ancient cradle-song in her native language, and then, as I drifted off to sleep, began to tell me a story.

"Miriam," she said, "you are a woman now, and I want to tell you about the great mother ... the story of woman. Men think that they rule the earth, but the earth rules them, and the earth is a woman; she bleeds like a woman; like a woman, she gives birth. Do you want me to tell you these things?"

"It sounds," I said, my mind already drifting from some potion she had brewed for me, "like abomination."

"Listen, listen." She took her hand from my brow. I snuggled into the pallet, drew the sheet over myself to shut out the moonlight that streamed in from a window high above, almost to the ceiling. "What do those rabbis now? They are men. Before ever there were men, there was the earth."

She started to tell me some tale about a mother goddess wandering the earth in search of a son ... about a king who was also a cornstalk ... about a god torn to pieces by wild priestesses, his blood running into the earth and seeding the world with renewed life ... she talked of ancient rites, celebrated in these hills before ever the Chosen came out of Egypt, ceremonies of uncontrolled lust where the gods came down and mated with wanton women ... I had heard such tales before, and paid it no mind now, for she was after all only a slave. She kept saying, "Time to know the truth, time for you to awaken," but I thought her a sad deluded thing, for all that she lavished more love on me than either of my parents; but that is a common failing in slaves, who in themselves have nothing to live for, and must glean their identity from the lives of others.

Still, that night, I dreamed....

There were the hills. Two hills that reeked of olives and goat dung. Two hills, two communities, an hour's brisk walk apart: Nazareth, so hidebound, Sepphoris, so Greek ... our house an uneasy hybrid of the two ... I dreamed of soaring above the hills into the moonlit sky ... of flitting through the tops of the olive trees ... I dreamed of the slave-woman's hilltop orgies, of naked bodies, of kings who were also cornstalks ... of Pantera, who had dared to touch me, comfort me, a niddah, unclean.   Pantera without his cuirass, wreathed in dry corn. Pantera reaching out his hand to me like the grizzled Jupiter in the forum at Sepphoris.

Such a pretty girl....

Sweating, I found myself awake long before dawn. The night sang to me through the high window. I called for the slave, but she was not there; perhaps, now that I was unclean, she was not allowed to lay her rush mat down beside my chest of cedarwood crammed with unworn clothes and unmended toys.

I don't know why; I was not usually restless at night; my mother always said that I was perfect when I slept, my arms folded neatly, a half-smile on my face; tonight, though, I could not sleep.

I slowly pushed open the door. There was Ruth, in a snoring heap just past the threshold. I tiptoed past her. The air was close and dank until I stepped into the atrium. There was only a puddle in the fountain — my mother always made sure we were frugal — but in the moonlight it sparkled like a circle of silver. The fragrance of roses almost overwhelmed the everpresent aroma of crushed olives.

And there was my centurion, transformed by moonlight into an idol of brass; he was naked, his bright skin dappled by the shadows of the rose bushes; he gleamed with the oil that he was even now scraping from himself with a little bronze strigil.

As I have said, my family was a little Greek, but not enough to be accustomed to casual nudity; in the matter of nakedness we were as old-fashioned as anyone in Nazareth. I had never stood this close to a naked grown man; to tell the truth, I could have reached out and grazed his shoulder as he sat, intent, on the stone bench.

I know I should have felt shame, but I had already had my fill of shame for the day, so I just stood there, staring. He was an alien being. His foreskin was particularly unnerving.

"How long have you been standing

there?"

I started. Of course he had seen me; he always saw me; there was no point in hiding.

"You'd better not scream; you're in enough of a pickle as it is. Imagine that! Do you think *I* startled you into having your period? Rather an honor, really. What's your name?"

"M-miriam," I said.

"Well, Miriam ... I'm doing this in the dead of night because there aren't a whole lot of amenities in this shithole of a village ... not even a proper bath-house. I know you people think it's vulgar to take one's clothes off, but it's better than having no personal hygiene at all, like all the wild prophets we have to round up from time to time around these parts."

"I've never seen a Roman before," I said in my most careful Greek.

He chuckled. "I'm no more Roman than you are, Miriam; I'm from Ephesus. Have you heard of Ephesus? That's where the Great Goddess lives — she's one of the seven wonders of the world, you know. Never been to Rome, can't even speak Latin; got my citizenship though, second generation. But then again, we are all Roman; the whole world's in Rome."

"*We're* not," I said.   "We have our own king."

"Who is most happy to grovel before Caesar, since Caesar has given him Judaea to civilize — now *there's* an uphill battle. He's a strange man, your Idumaean king — he is civilized enough to worship the Mother as well as this Jewish god, yet he's crueler even than the Romans. Do you go into Sepphoris much?"

"My father doesn't think it's a good idea —"

"You should contrive to go. Get a little culture into you before that egghead puts the chains on you and sets you to making babies."

It was amazing, the way he talked, the things he talked about — I couldn't understand half of what he said, but then his voice did have that music to it....

"The mysteries, too," Pantera went on. "The mysteries ... in the hills ... you could come to them ... the slave will take you ... she's a woman, she understands. The first time, you shouldn't let a mere mortal touch you; you should give yourself to the gods...."

"They do that in Babylon," I said. "The women there are all whores."

He laughed out loud — I suppose I must have sounded *very* naive to him — then checked himself quickly, fearful perhaps of wakening my family. He looked right into my eyes. I was only a girl, and there he sat, looking, sounding, smelling of a vast and unknown world. "Miriam, Miriam, you could even become mother to a god," he said, and caressed me again, lightly, on the cheek. "The gods could touch you ... even as I touch you."

"You shouldn't do that," I said, "you'll have to be purified."

"Imagine that! Mother to the god ... like Semele, like Maia, like Pasiphaë."

"Who are those people?" I asked him.

"Each was an ordinary woman touched by the fire of godhead. An ordinary woman who partook of the nature of the Great Mother. An ordinary woman who became mother to the god."

He used the same words Paul was to use forty years later, that bleak cold day when he burst into my ugly unswept house, though in years to come those better versed in Greek were to find a more elegant word for what they wanted me to be: *theotokos,* god-bearer.

4

"... and of course," Paul added, "you were a virgin."

This time I positively hooted. "Paul, you silly little man ... what century are we in? I'll count them for you, since you're a Roman citizen, you say ... we are in the Eighth Century of the self-styled greatest nation in history. Not to mention thousands of years since Abraham! You say you've seen Rome, but even a cast-off hag like me knows that we live in an age of wonders, of scientific marvels, of straight Roman roads that link the whole world, of monumental technologies ... how are these enlightened Gentiles of yours going to believe such a stupid idea?"

"Because, mother, they need to believe it ... and because by the time I'm through with this idea it will be the truth."

"But I've had seven children!" This was

too outlandish to be credited. "Will you say that Lord sewed my maidenhead back up seven times? Or will you pretend the other children never existed? That might be hard, with my secondborn James in Jerusalem even now, persisting in all this insanity."

"Mother," said Paul, "we may live in a gleaming new world, but we're alienated. No one believes in the gods anymore — except here, of course, beyond the outer edge of the civilized world.   Religion means something here. People will die for it. Now back there, in the Empire's heart, there are those who would die for something to die for. The heart doesn't want a new road or a new aqueduct — the heart wants a miracle — the heart wants redemption — the heart wants love."

"You mean to say, Paul, that *you* want love. Who do you love, Paul?"

He jerked his head away from me. I think he was suddenly in tears. I knew then that he was running away from something; that there was an aching emptiness inside him; a whole world of love might not suffice to fill that void. I pitied him. It's hard to avoid being a mother.

I knew he would change the subject, and he did.

"Virginity," he said.

"I'm dying to know how you plan to pull that one off."

"Miriam, bear with me," he said, pulling out the wax tablet I'd seen him scribbling on beside the well. "It's all a matter of midrash. All of the present world can be found predicted in the Law and the Prophets, if we only know where to look. Let me show you what I've uncovered —"

He handed me the wax tablet. "You expect me to read that?" I said. "I'm a woman."

"Roman women read," he said. His brow furrowed in puzzlement. "Why, in Alexandria, even Jewish women —" He must have caught my dark look, so he simply began to declaim: "Behold, a virgin shall conceive...."

"This is nonsense," I said. "This comes of only reading the Prophets in Greek ..."

"You know the passage?"

"I can't read, but I *was* married to the Carpenter; I would think a bit of book-learning would have rubbed off. First of all, you're quoting the whole thing out of context. Isaiah was prophesying that the line of King Ahaz wouldn't die out, and furthermore your Greek may say *parthenos,* a virgin, but the real text says *almah,* an unmarried woman.   With midrashes like these, you wouldn't last five minutes in a rabbinical debate."

It was odd the way Paul looked at me. I knew the look well — after all, I've had five sons and two daughters. It's the look you get from one of your children when he's been caught with his hand in the sweetmeats — and he comes up with a whopper of an excuse that's so gloriously farfetched that you have to stifle your laughter before you punish him. Winsome, that's it.

"Oh, come on, mother," he said. "It's not you I have to convince."

Then and there, I decided that I liked Paul after all. I've always been good with little boys. All, that is, except my wayward firstborn, poor mad Joshua, the boy who was always ready to forgive his enemies, yet never could never bring himself to forgive his mother.

But that's for later.

As for my virginity....

5

After a week, I entered my ritual bath as an unclean girl, and emerged a purified woman. The slaves treated me a little differently; my father kept even more distance than he used to; and Joseph came calling more often, though I still was not allowed to be alone with him.

Nor was I alone with the centurion, who presently went to Sepphoris, the proper quarters having finally been readied for him. I watched him ride down the hill from the door of my house. I did not think I would see him again, but that night I did, in a strange dream that once more woke me and made me fear to go back to sleep.

I dreamed of his eyes. I dreamed of the moon. I dreamed of him dancing on the hillside, of the silvery light and the bronze skin dappled by the shadows of olive-branches; I dreamed of him becoming an olive-tree, of the branches jutting from his forehead like antlers; in my dream I tossed and turned, and awake tossed and turned still more, and rubbed those Greek linen sheets against my skin, and felt a strange and fiery tingling from within myself, did not recognize the feeling, only knew somehow I should feel ashamed.

Nightly the dreams grew more intense. I dreaded going to sleep, begged Ruth to tell me more of her silly stories, only they seemed to fuel the dreams; pulled my old doll back out of the chest, mourned her missing limbs and cracked neck, slammed her hard against the wall, decided she was dead and I should bury her....

Which, the next night, I did. In the atrium, under a rose-bush. I scooped up a few handfuls of earth with my bare hands, and placed Shoshana carefully in her cradle of dirt.

She was not a person anymore. She never had been, had she? I popped the remaining eye of lapis from her face; the two eyes were the only part of value anyway. Then I covered the doll up hastily. I started to go back to my room, but in my path stood the immense bulk of the Anatolian slave woman.

Arms crossed, a dour look; I cowered a little, for all that I was her mistress. "Burying the doll, I suppose," she said severely.

"But she was only a graven image," I said. "She had no soul. I was wrong to hold her so dear."

Ruth took me in her arms, and hugged me — she smelled of sweat and vinegar — and said, "You really *have* become a woman, little mistress. I was right to come looking for you tonight. Not a sound now. You're coming with me."

"Where?"

"To the top of the hill," she said. "It's time for you to learn a new song."

"Why?" I said.

"Be quiet," she said. She had never taken this tone with me before. She used the voice with authority, for I obeyed her without thinking, and let her lead me by the hand through the kitchen, through the triclinium, to the antechamber, to the front door of my father's house....

And before I knew it, we were actually outside. There was a conspiracy, it seemed, to let me leave. The night-watchman was dozing by the gate. In the kitchen, the cook and her boy were snoring. Slaves have a secret language; they're always conniving with each other, always know what's really going on.   Past our house, the dwellings grew smaller as the hill grew steeper.

Now this was the oddest thing: Nazareth by night is a dead place. The Romans say Sepphoris is dead at night, but by that they mean that only a few taverns and brothels have all-night service, and you can't find a link-boy to light your way down the alleys after, say, the fourth hour of the evening. Nazareth is like a graveyard by the third hour. And yet tonight things were different.

Here and there a slender shadow darted from doorway to doorway. Always going uphill. No one had torches. No one spoke. Ruth clutched my hand. We walked in bold strides, impelled by some strange urgency; I could almost smell it in the air. "In your house," Ruth said, in between big, noisy breaths, "I am a slave. But on the hilltop I'm a high priestess. The wind and the earth know my name. The moon sings through my lips."

And now I was in terror, because her words reeked of abomination. Yet the fascination kept me walking. I was only thirteen. Soon I would be married. Had I not buried my childhood less than an hour ago? I deserved a little adventure. Maybe I wouldn't see Rome or even Ephesus or Damascus, for that matter. Well, at least I would stand on the hilltop with my slave woman, and see a little further out into the world, even if only a mile or two....

Soon we left Nazareth behind. That is very easy to do. A wind sprang up. The dirt road petered out. We negotiated our way through a flock of sheep. The hill grew steeper, rockier; the stones sparkled in the full moon. Ruth moved purposefully; I had never seen her be so agile; I can barely keep up. She knew every turn, every foothold. At length, passing through a clump of trees, we reached a flat clearing. What I saw appalled me, yet I could not look away.

The women were dressed only in leaves and skins. They were drunk. They danced, they swayed, they sang in unknown tongues. There was a shrilling music of flute and drum. The women were in a loose circle, and some held hands, and though most were clearly foreigners, I recognized some of the most important women in Nazareth as well ... and there were men. At first I did not see them because they were clothed in the bark of trees, and they held branches in their arms and waved them slowly ... I realized we had not passed through a grove at all, that all had been men ... and in the center of the circle was tall woman, almost as tall as a house, only she was a woman made entirely of sheaves of corn lashed together with ropes ... an idol! and the men were calling out to her, naming her with many names, Demeter, Ashtaroth, Cybele, or simply Mother. They spoke many languages: Greek and Latin I had a smattering of, but stranger tongues than that too, twangings, yowlings, guttural mutterings.

I felt a terrible dread, and yet the drumming quickened my pulse and filled me with the urge to dance....

"I know that woman there —" I started to say.

Ruth shushed me. "We have no names tonight. This is the night I have been preparing you for, the rituals of spring."

"Some abomination brought here by the Romans —"

"No, girl — be careful what you call abomination — these rites were celebrated in these hills long before Moses came out of Egypt, and they will be celebrated when your people are just a memory —"

Never had I understood before that Ruth, a slave woman, had her own past, her own people. I had always thought of her as part of us, a lowly part, yet fully of our family.

"These are witches!" I suddenly exclaimed. Several women looked around at me angrily. Did not the Tanakh say, "Thou shalt not suffer a witch to live?" But these were modern times. I looked at Ruth, afraid of her for the first time, for all that I had suckled at her breast. Were those quaint folk tales of her homeland, the ones that sometimes gave me nightmares, more than just childish stories? "Are you a witch?" I asked her, softly, for I did not want to attract more ireful glances from the other women.

"Wine!" she cried, and handed me a cup, from which, out of nervousness and fear, I drank deeply, not realizing till later that this wine was undiluted, and had a bitter aftertaste.   The wine was cool, and the wind on the hill was chilly, and I felt the wine's inner warmth seep into me, and presently I too was swaying with the others ... I do not know when I found myself stripped to my tunic, or when the branches found their way into my hands, but I was waving them to and fro, and the unfamiliar words came haltingly from my lips, and knew I was praying to some unknown power ... *mother,* I found myself whispering, and tears sprang to my eyes, for my own mother was not with me, never held me, never wanted me close; instead, I had this slave woman for a mother, holding me in the night, telling me forbidden stories, even letting herself be whipped for my sake.   I was crying, and flushed from the wine, and intoxicated by the alien music, and at length became aware that I now understood the words of the song: *The king must die. The king must die. The king must die.*

The men, in their animal skins and antler-like branches, now marched in a solemn procession. They led a lamb into the center of the circle. One crushed a crown of thorns down on the lamb's tender head.   Blood ran into its eyes.   Another threw on the lamb's back a cloak of royal purple.   On either side of the lamb stood a man holding a burning torch high, and behind this tableau stood the tall goddess made of corn.

The drumming sped up and crescendoed. Suddenly, in a frenzy, the women swooped down on the lamb.   I was among them.   I could not help myself.   We were ripping the flesh from the animal, heedless of its squeals.   There was blood everywhere.   My hands were slick with it, my face matted with blood and pieces of fur.   It was over before I even fully realized what I had done, and then we were trampling the shredded flesh into the ground, shouting *Seed the world! Seed the world! Seed the world!*

I was seized with anger and joy all at once.   The trampling became a dance. And Ruth, dancing beside me, ululating, seemed possessed.   In the house, she was a woman who always carried a cloud of melancholy around with her; now she was driven by an ecstasy that had to come from some supernatural source.

Then came new words: *The king has*

come to life in the belly of the earth. The king has come to renew the waters of life. The king is the god is the sky is the sower of life. The womb of the corn-goddess opened up, and from it stepped a naked man. A man soaked in blood, shaggy and grizzled. A man I knew. Oh, he was beautiful to me; he was terrifying; he was everything I imagined in a heathen god. As he moved slowly to the center of the circle which represented the world, flaming torches were cast into the woman of corn, so that she burned behind him and made his gleaming flesh glitter like polished brass. And his eyes stared across the throng, stared right into my own ... or so I fancied, I a thirteen-year-old girl new to womanhood, new to the pull of passion. "Pantera!" I cried. "Oh, Pantera!"

"Shush, girl! We have no names here," Ruth said. "That is no man. It's the god who returns in triumph after harrowing hell. This is the rebirth of the world."

Pantera spread his arms wide, and then began the actual rites of fertility — when the men and women shed their garments and rushed inside the sacred circle to cleave to one another, nameless all, vessels of a primeval force. And I too, not knowing that this would signal the death of innocence, rushed to the center, straight into the arms of the creature who had haunted my dreams.

He enveloped me. The heat of the burning goddess made our sweat run, melted me into him. His eyes were the sea. He invaded what no man had invaded and I did not resist. The drums pounded. There was blood everywhere; I never knew one animal had so much blood. Then came a sharp interior pain, and my own blood mingled with the blood of the sacrifice, and I screamed, but this corn-god hushed me, stilled me, lulled me, lowered me into a profound and peaceful place within myself ... I closed my eyes and entered a moist warm darkness.

I opened them only once, to see another woman I knew well, whom I had never seen naked, writhing, whinnying, bucking above the ever-changing sea of flesh ... "Mother?" I whispered, before descending once again into a featureless sheol that was neither bliss nor terror.

***

I saw her face again when I woke up. I expected to see it red with rage, but there was an unwonted concern; she was mopping my brow with a cool cloth, and Ruth was fanning me. They did not know I was awake, I suppose, for they spoke about me as if I wasn't there.

"I told you she was too young," my mother said. "Next year would have been soon enough."

"Mistress, you know as well as I do that next year she will already have been married away from us, living who knows where. And the mysteries *are* important. Men have so much in this land, and we have nothing. …"

"Oh, I should have you beaten."

"As you wish, mistress."

"Why didn't you warn her not to walk right into the center of the circle?"

"You know she did what she had to do," said Ruth. "The Mother called her."

"Idolatry! They are empty rituals ... nothing more."

"Mistress, if they were truly empty, your men would not go to such pains to condemn them, to call for such harsh penalties."

"They may call for them, but no one exacts them. King Herod himself — only a half-Jew, of course, but he does countenance such rites — no one wants the crops to fail."

"Then they are not empty, Mistress," said Ruth, with relentless logic.

"But she's been feverish for three days!" my mother said, and for the first time I realized how long I had been in that alien limbo.

I realized, too, that my mother loved me. That was the strangest thing of all. If this heathen ritual had brought me to this awareness, surely it could not have been utterly evil. "Mother?" I said softly.

But seeing I was awake, my mother turned dour again. "You'd better not breathe a word," she said. "This is women's business. Joseph won't know, neither will your father. As for your maidenhead, there are ways to make sure you bleed copiously on your wedding night; no need to worry."

"But mother —" I said.

"Be quiet, or your fever will never go away … oh, you will be the death of me! … lie still and let Ruth fan you. There! You'll be as good as new by tomorrow."

"As long as she's not pregnant," said Ruth, very quietly, to herself.

"Pregnant! She'd better not be! You gave her the appropriate potions, didn't you?" said my mother. "If she is, I will make sure you are sold to the sleaziest brothel in Sepphoris."

Gradually I sank back into a daze. I thought of the moonlight. I thought of the centurion. I thought of the blazing goddess, crumbling into ash. As I slid deeper into my dream, I could faintly hear my mother mutter, above the roar of the flaming corn: "Pregnant! Pregnant! The very idea!"

6

As it turned out, I was.

And so began the journey that was to lead me to this meeting with a strange little man who claimed to have spoken to my son, yet never saw him in the flesh.

And other meetings, with people and be-ings stranger even than Saul of Tarsus. The Empress of the World. The Eternal Virgin Moon. Living gods and dying kings.

Did God plant Joshua in my womb? On the face of it, it was a ludicrous proposition. A heathen ritual in a rural community, with ignorant villagers and thrill-seekers from the pagan town on the next hill, presided over by a self-styled priestess who was really a slave ... was this a respectable venue for an encounter with the one whose name we dare not speak? And yet is God not every-where? Did the things Paul say to me make a twisted sort of sense, or was it merely that he was so skilled at packing paganism into a Jewish box?

They were not pleased to learn of my condition....

***

I was vomiting in my room when my future husband came calling. Ruth told me that I had to attend a meeting, but when I reached the triclinium my mother said, "Sit in the corner, child, and don't say a word. Try to be invisible."

I did. I tried to curl up behind a low table laden with fruit, but I couldn't hide from the Carpenter's stare. It was not the kind of baleful look my parents gave me when I had done something wrong; it was as though I had somehow wounded him; and this was strange, for I hardly knew him, and had never meant to hurt him.

I kept my eyes downcast during most of the conversation, but now and then I stole a glance. My future husband was no older than the centurion, but there were lines around his eyes and he was already a little gray, and he stooped a little, as scholars tend to.

My mother kept murmuring, "Oh, this is

a disaster, this is a disaster." None of them would look at me, except Joseph. My father seemed crushed, and it was Ruth, strangely enough, who seemed to offer an endless list of solutions. "The problem could be made to disappear completely," she began, "if we go and visit a certain woman in Sepphoris. ..."

"What?" my father cried in a sudden passion. "And pile abomination on abomination?"

"Don't be so self-righteous, Joachim," my mother said, "she is only trying to help. She doesn't know what's proper and what's abomination."

"The question is not whether to kill the child," my father said. "The question is whether the Carpenter will accept his wine in a broken vessel."

"Abomination upon abomination is not the end of the world," my mother said, "if no one finds out about it."

"What do you say, Joseph?" my father said.

There was silence. Joseph was, after all, the final arbiter on this matter. No wonder my parents had such an air of helplessness.

The Carpenter did not answer them for a long while; he continued to stare at me. At length, he said, "There are always two in a marriage. If Miriam loves another, I will not compel her."

"That's not the point —" my mother began, and I realized at once that neither Joseph nor my father knew anything of the escapade that made me pregnant.

"Then the father won't come forward, nor will Miriam accuse anyone?" Joseph asked. "Did someone force you? Was it a stranger? A member of the occupying forces? Was it a Samaritan?" He never raised his voice, and with each putative candidate my parents grew paler and more rigid. And then he asked me, "Miriam, do you not love me?"

To which I gave the only reply that a well-brought-up girl can give: "How should I know, Carpenter? We are not even fully married yet. Older and wiser women have always told me it takes years to learn to love one's husband."

Nervously, my father began helping himself to a plate of Babylonian sweetmeats.

"As for the *neduniyah* —"he began.

"Don't be so crass, Joachim!" my mother

hissed, "Of course he'll return the dowry, if he sets her aside." She stared pointedly at the Carpenter, to make the point that Joseph could ill afford to lose my father's generous neduniyah.

"Then you'll take her," my mother said.

"I won't go back on my word," said my future husband, "though none of this is particularly pleasing to me. But let me add that the Torah does not specifically forbid abortion; it merely spells out the compensation that must be paid to a woman's husband should a man assault that woman and incidentally abort her unborn child. So the idea that it is abomination could be argued either way."

"Then you want her to go to that sorceress in Sepphoris —" said my father.

"That is not for me to say," Joseph said, "but I will not go back on my word."

"So you will go through with the final solemnization of the marriage," my mother said.

"I have given my word," said the Carpenter.

But he would not come out and say simply *yes*; and so my mother, terrified that he would change his mind, decided to send me to Sepphoris in secret, without telling my father, accompanied only by Ruth, to seek the help of a certain old woman.   That woman's name was Xanthe; though she had adopted a Greek name, as did anyone with any pretension to being civilized, she was really a Babylonian, a devotee of Ishtar, which was another guise of the Great Mother.

Before we reached her house, however, our path took us past the gymnasium....

7

Sepphoris, a scant hour's walk from Nazareth, had always been forbidden me. It was down one hill and up another; by donkey it was a little slower, for the animal was old and often had to be coaxed. It was my father who insisted on the donkey.

We started long before dawn, for my mother did not want me seen, and we were both veiled, more veiled than was necessary for decency. I was glad it was not yet day; the layers of clothing were stifling.

Sepphoris was a minor showcase of King Herod's Hellenic miracle. All Galilee and Judaea knew how this ambitious half-Jew, a commoner to boot, had convinced Augustus Caesar that he was the one to transform those stiffnecked desert dwellers into civilized subjects of the Emperor. Good Roman plumbing and decent Greek drama were now commonplace, as were crucifixions. We saw a few outside the gates of Sepphoris. Each had the *causa poenae* inscribed above his head, but neither of us could read, so we did not know if these men were dying for some serious crime, or whether they had merely displeased someone.

"Don't worry, little mistress." Ruth said as we entered the town. "One way or another, we will take care of you."

Sepphoris was really just a tawdry frontier town — I know that now — but to my young eyes it seemed a spectacle beyond belief. In the forum were vendors of trinkets and pottery and — most astonishing of all — forbidden foods, skewers of succulent pork, platters of shrimp; I saw Romans, Greeks, Egyptians, and Persians jabbering they devoured these unclean foods, whose odor sickened me to my stomach; I was even more amazed to see Ruth buy a sausage for a bronze lepton and consume it with relish. "What a relief," she said, turning to me and beaming broadly, "to eat real food again."

"Where did you get that money?"

"I save a little," she said, "hoarding to buy my freedom. But on a day when I can eat a pork sausage, my freedom can wait...."

Already, within only a few weeks of losing my good girl status, I was experiencing a broadening of my world. And if the world could be this alien a scant hour's walk from my house, what further wonders must there be? I pondered this as we traversed the forum. A painted woman on a litter borne by Nubians ... a Babylonian god being paraded through the square, followed by drummers and conch-shell trumpeters ... a platform where chained monkeys, birds, and children sat, waiting to be auctioned ... and always the Romans, always on guard, always policing, always glowering, now and then stopping a man for questioning, now and then pulling someone from the crowd and dragging him away.

Ruth paused to ask the way, and then we took a side street, past a small temple of Venus, past the bloated façade of a public baths. They were wide streets — to me they seemed wide — with a sewer down the middle, and stepping stones at regular intervals so you could cross without soiling your garments.

Past the baths there was a building with an Ionic colonnade, and Ruth quickly whispered, "Look away, now, girl; there are things it's not proper for a nice Jewish girl to see —" which naturally made me look up and stare.

It was a marble courtyard lined with graven images — images of naked men in various states of indecent display. And there were men. They were as naked as the statues. And they were wrestling, chatting, walking arm on shoulder, rubbing each other down with oil and strigils, just as naturally and shamelessly as if they were fully clothed.

I gasped, which I should not have done, for they all turned to look, and then they started laughing.

"What's the fuss?" An authoritative figure entered the courtyard. He, too, was naked. It was Pantera. Not clothed in moonlight, not obscured by cornstalks or olive-branches ... I had never seen him this way, in the bright sun ... he was not the same. His body sagged in places. There was a white scar in his side. I couldn't help staring at it. He laughed. "Oh, just some Celtic spear," he said. "Judaea's not the only rough spot in the Empire, you know. Why did you come to Sepphoris?"

"To see a sorceress," I said.

Ruth elbowed me out of the way and whispered in Pantera's ear. He grew serious now. "No, no," he said. "We can't have that."

At that moment another man entered the courtyard. He was old, white-haired, weatherbeaten; he wore a white robe bordered with purple, a mark of some high rank among the Romans. Everyone in the courtyard deferred to him, although they did not prostrate themselves as people might in the court of Herod. I sensed power in him, and also compassion.

"Who is this?" he said. He had a soft voice, one used to having its slightest whim obeyed.

"Senator," said Pantera, "this is the Jewess Miriam, who bears in her womb the child of a god, conceived during the rituals of spring."

The old man's eyes sparkled. "Why," he said, "splendid, splendid. Greetings," he said to me, addressing me by a Latin form of my name, "Maria; it is said that a woman such as you is blessed above all other women; that she dwells in a state of divine grace; surely the gods are with you."

"Senator, this woman was on her way to see a sorceress; her mother doesn't believe her husband-to-be will see eye-to-eye with our interpretation of her pregnancy."

"I think, centurion, that you have more than a personal interest in this matter."

"Senator, you know we cannot speak of what happens during the mysteries...."

"Enough said. We shall save this child of the gods."

The senator clapped his hands. An im-pressive-looking eunuch — outweighing even the bulky Ruth — appeared as though by magic, He was holding a wax tablet and a stylus, and was poised to take notes.

"You will instruct the commander of the garrison to send a maniple of cavalry to the house of —"

"Joseph," said Ruth, "of Nazareth, known a the Carpenter."

"This Joseph, et cetera, and let this Joseph at once be apprehended and escorted — no, no, too highhanded, by Jupiter! — be *invited* to the quarters of the commander of the garrison of Sepphoris, to be interviewed by the Senator Gaius Proculus on matters concerning the populace of — oh, what province is this, now? — Galilee. Oh! And take another note — I'll sacrifice a pair of doves tomorrow at the temple of Venus, for a happy future for the child, you know," he explained. He smiled, and patted me benignly on the head. "That's all taken care of then," he said. "It's good work you're doing, Maria; bridging our two cultures, helping us all see eye to eye; we're all part of the grand scheme of things now, we've simply *got* to learn to live in harmony, and so on; you would agree, would you not?"

He paced along the colonnade expansively, not pausing for an answer. "You see, my dear," he went on, as I tried to keep up with him, flinging his arms this way and that, perhaps practicing for some great senatorial speech, "the Emperor has sent me on a fact-finding mission. There have been some very ugly rumors ... well, that that Herod fellow is getting a bit too full of himself, putting down dissent too viciously, overtaxing the natives, and so on. Killing off one's own children to avoid dynastic disagreement ... that's an internal affair and all that, but it does indicate a certain lack of ... proper civilized values.   It's been said that it would be better to be Herod's pig than his son.   The Emperor is considering some rather radical alternatives ... such as running the province directly from Rome with a senatorially-appointed procurator, or splitting off Galilee from Judaea to streamline the bureaucracy ... anyhow, you see, my dear girl, you must understand that even the little person can play a *very* important role in bringing about the Pax Romana. I'm proud of you. Hail Caesar!"

A chorus of *Hail Caesars* ran around the courtyard, and the eunuch scurried away to summon the troops.

***

And so it was that I did not see Xanthe after all; and this was well, for later I heard stories that turned my stomach; of women rent asunder, made forever barren; of deaths, even. Instead, I was escorted to the house of the garrison commander, where the senator was lodging; I was told to wait in an anteroom, and a plate of delicacies placed before me, which I dared not touch for fear that they might be unclean; I was told nothing of what to expect. No one sat with me. Ruth sat in attendance at my feet, but for once she seemed intimidated; she said nothing at all.

It was almost the ninth hour when Joseph came storming into the antechamber.

"Well," he cried, "I refused their money. I have that much self-respect at least. A thousand sesterces! What sorcery is this, that an illiterate girl who has never set foot outside her village can make Rome herself offer me a thousand sesterces?"

"I don't know what you mean," I said.

"Do you know what they threatened next?" he said. "If I didn't legitimize the child, they said they might even crucify me."

"That kindly senator said that?"

"You'd think the Empire would have something better to do than play the village marriage broker," he railed. "Who is the father, Miriam? It must be someone important. It was a Roman, wasn't it? I should kill him."

"Don't, Joseph —" I began.

"I won't," he said. "It seems we are to be married, and I am to name the child myself, ensuring its legitimacy."

"They told you to do that?"

"Why will no one tell me who the father is?" he said. "I tried to get them to tell me, and they began laughing. They told me the gods had done it. One of them — may the Lord forgive me for letting such impiety fall upon my ears — one of them even intimated that the Lord God of Hosts himself was the father, and had the temerity to refer to him by the Unspeakable Name, the Holy Tetragrammaton!"

He was very distraught. I could understand why, if the idolaters had been making light of our religion, and daring to utter the Name that may not be uttered, except by the high priest, and that only once a year, and the drums and the trumpets must play at maximum volume so that the sound of the name does not fall upon the ears of the unworthy.

"Joseph," I said, "they are only heathens. You are my Lord. If you tell me to leave your sight for ever, I will do so. If you tell me to seek out this abortionist, I will. If you take me as your wife, that is my duty. But I beg you, if you name the child and thus acknowledge him as your own, don't let the child know that we plotted to kill him in the womb; love him as your own. Promise me that at least."

I said this because I had come to realize that this thing inside me was no abstraction. It would soon be a human being, one who would call me *ima, ima,* and suckle at my breasts ... for much as I loved Ruth I did not want my child to have a wet-nurse; that special closeness between a child and his source of nourishment, I did not want to relinquish, for I knew that my mother and I would never be bonded as closely as were I and the slave woman.

I wanted the child. I wanted to be loved for my own sake. Everyone who had discussed the child's fate had done so as though my opinion did not even count. But while they argued and fretted, my love for the child within had been fanned from a guttering flame to a blaze.

Whether his father was god or man, I would never give him up. No matter how high and mighty they were, how many airs they put on, how many noble speeches they gave, these men were never going to be mothers. In a world controlled by emperors and centurions and husbands, here at last was a territory I could call my own.

II
Flight

1

This time the house was not quite so ugly, and it was bigger. The house belonged to another Miriam, who had become infatuated with my son James and the zealous excesses of his community; the house was next to, but was not quite as unpleasant as, an insula, which was what the Romans called the low-rent tenements they built to house the transient workers who always traveled in their wake. When my sons were not at this Miriam's house, they lodged at another place belonging to our family patron, Joseph of Arimathea, who had many houses in Jerusalem; he himself generally preferred the balmier climate of Caesarea, or was away on business, in Alexandria or all the way in Celtic Britannia, buying tin; since Joshua's death my family had come to rely more and more upon his charity.

I did not know why Paul insisted on my coming to Jerusalem with him. I did not really understand why he needed my physical presence in order to announce his revolutionary religion. After all, he had not really asked for my consent. He had not won my endorsement — how could I endorse what was so patently implausible?

Years ago, I had told James the same thing ... that he a was fool and would end up like his brother. Yet I did want to see him again. One never stops worrying about one's children. It doesn't matter how old they get.

As we drew closer to the city, Paul seemed to get more and more nervous. He lay with his back to the side of he oxcart, muttering to himself; sometimes he seemed to be talking to someone. I leaned on a large cool amphora. The owner of the cart traveled frequently to Jerusalem; he was a wine merchant, and had an irregular schedule of deliveries to the better houses in the city. It was an odd way to travel, but Paul, it seemed, had a knack for finding un-orthodox ways to get where he needed to go, often without paying.

How had he managed it this time?

"Oh," he said, "I told him what a precious cargo he carried." So perhaps, without my permission or knowledge, the rumors of my semi-divine status had already started.

***

I knew Jerusalem well by now, though almost every memory I have of that city is one I would rather forget. The first time I entered Jerusalem, I remember thinking, Well, Sepphoris is only a village after all ... fancy that. Since then, I have seen Rome, so I know that even Jerusalem can be seen as a parochial little border town with few of the amenities that the self-styled civilized are accustomed to.

We had not quite reached the Jaffa gate; the walls that had failed to keep out the Romans loomed in the distance, but the road was already jammed with food-stalls and souvenir vendors. Here and there, a condemned criminal, strung up above the commotion, added a whiff of putrefaction to the sultry air. Paul asked the wine-merchant to let us off in front of a carpet vendor's pavilion; dusty and sweaty, we emerged, as unlikely a traveling pair as one might imagine.

At the stall, a dirty little boy swatted flies and absently stuffed himself with dates. His master was busy with a customer, larding on the obsequies while furiously trying to steer him toward the more expensive stacks.

Paul shied a lepton at the boy's nose. He snapped to attention, smiled shyly, and said, "Oh, you're back."

"There's another lepton for you if fetch me Barnabas."

"Can't," he said. "I'm minding the rugs."

"I've been traveling all day," said Paul, "and I really need to see him."

"How many lepta?"

"Two," said Paul, "and a beating thrown in."

As the boy scurried off, I asked Paul why we did not go straight to the house where my son was staying. Wasn't that the plan ... to make an appearance at the apostles' little community house, present Paul's radical vision to them, and have them all immediately switch to his new religion? That — absurdly enough — was how easy Paul had made it sound — had even convinced me to come with him, a step I was already beginning to regret — had appealed, I suppose, to my motherly instincts. "You're not telling me everything, Paul," I said.

"No, mother," he said, "I'm not."

But he seemed reluctant to explain further, and meanwhile the carpet vendor, had finished his business and was now being introduced to me. "Ah, the mother," he said, bowing. "When the mother decides to take charge, things really start to move."

"Take charge of what?" I said.

"Why, mother," he said, "of the great new age that now is dawning in the world." I think, for a moment, he was wondering whether he should kneel. Then, nervously, he turned to Paul and said, "You see, the tent you sold me last year still holds, but you might want to sell me some new pegs, one or two of them seem to have corroded. ..."

It was thus that I learned Paul's actual

profession ... no rabbi as he wanted to be known, as I had already figured out from his incomplete knowledge of the scriptures ... a tentmaker. Why not a tentmaker? My son had recruited peasants as well as rich men ... fishermen, whores, merchants ... he was more of a democrat than any Athenian, if the truth were told.

Now came the man they called Barnabas, a man as lanky as Paul was squat, who spoke no Aramaic at all, though he was a Jew, being from Cyprus; so the conversation continued in Greek. He was distressed to see Paul. "What are you doing here?" he said.

"I have to see James and the others," said Paul.

"They're going to kill you," said Barnabas.

"No," said Paul. "I've had a revelation. I've had an encounter with Joshua bar Joseph, and he wants me to come to Jerusalem and take my place among the apostles."

"Does a fox take his place among chickens? No one's going to buy that story; even I don't, and I'm your friend. Did the Sadducees send you to infiltrate the community and turn in the ringleaders? They couldn't

have picked a less suitable person. Everyone knows you hate the followers of Joshua
bar Joseph. Everyone knows you disagree
with everything he stood for. And everyone's still angry with you about Stephen."

"I was afraid of this," Paul said, sitting
himself down on the nearest pile of rugs.
He was pouting. I knew that look well. He
was used to getting his own way, and diffi-
cult when crossed. I had raised five boys —
not always all that successfully — and one
thing you learn is no matter how old they
get, they're always little boys; boys don't
grow up; growing up is a woman's job; it
comes with carrying the water jar and
pounding the laundry on the river-bank.

The little boy came to me and shyly prof-
fered a bowl of cool water; I drank, and tried
to shake the dust out of my traveling-cloak.

Paul said, "Barnabas, I've had many a bad
throw of the dice in life. Just how bad, I
hope never to have to tell you. My father
raised me in silence, you know. Books were
my friends; I never found a woman; and
then came my worst misfortune; there came
a war for the soul of the world, and I came
in on the wrong side. But now I've had a vi-

sion. Joshua has spoken to me. I have to tell his brothers about it. I have to spread the good news everywhere ... to every city, every country of the world."

"The world? But not every city in the world has Jews."

"The message," sad Paul, "isn't just for the Jews anymore. It's for all men."

It was a simple sentence, but one that took everyone's breath away. I do not think my son Joshua ever conceived a vision quite so catholic as this bowlegged little man's. I knew my son James was not going to like it, and it seemed there was bad feeling already between the two of them.

"And this time," Paul added, "my luck has held. I've thrown a Venus, and I'm going to collect the whole kitty."

My knowledge of gambling was limited, but people who speak Greek love to use gambling metaphors; I knew that a Venus was the highest score you could get in dice. And what *was* that highest score? Paul was pointing at me. I, Miriam, was to be Paul's secret weapon. Once again — as when I was pregnant, and my elders argued over my fate — I was to be made the repository of all sorts of profound meaning and symbolism, but I was not to be consulted.

"You mean Miriam," Barnabas said. "But the sons of Miriam are not well known for listening to their mother...."

True enough. If they had, they wouldn't both be dead.

"Try it this time," said Paul.

Of course, I had not agreed to say anything to James. Undoubtedly he would not listen anyway, or he would draw his own meaning from anything I did say.

At any rate, I finally entered the city in the company of the two men, and after a winding uphill walk through jostling, odoriferous crowds — always, somewhere in the picture, the policing Roman army standing watch — reached the bigger, less ugly house of Miriam of Jerusalem.

It was one of those houses with two stories, built around an open courtyard with a private well. The gate was open, and Paul charged straight in without pausing to touch the mezuzah.

"He's very modern," Barnabas commented drily, which was of course a euphemism for *very Greek*. It was odd that even Barnabas should say so, since he knew neither Aramaic nor Hebrew.

The courtyard was much as I remembered it from the madness of the Festival of Weeks, a few years earlier, when the apostles worked themselves into so frenzied a fervor that they began babbling in strange tongues, an event that had grown in the telling to the status of a miracle. The crowd was not quite so big, nor quite so animated; but there were the usual lepers, slaves, widows, and sick men with crutches; among them moved Joshua's old friends, comforting, laying on their hands, casting out devils — in short, doing the kind of work that holy men do everywhere. They worked the crowd with a sort of chaotic purposefulness, as the spirit moved them, I suppose. A few, screaming that they had been healed, ran joyfully about. In one corner, Simon Cephas, nicknamed the Rock, whom Joshua had trusted above all the others, not even excepting his own brother, was delivering a sermon which echoed the purifying sentiments his crucified rabbi had taught — the message of the Essenes and of John the Baptist, using plain speech, cutting through the clutter of scripture to the compassionate heart of the Torah.

When James came down the steps, I marveled at how much he had grown to resemble his brother — pudgier and stouter to be sure, and without those blue-gray eyes that betokened Joshua's profane — no, his divine — origins — yet with the same otherworldly look, half godlike, half insane. This was a puzzlement, because when Joshua was alive, James always did everything he could to look and act as different as he could from his brother.

He did not see me at first. I am adept at blending with the shadows. He saw Paul, and I knew at once that he was not pleased.

"You're not supposed to be here," he shouted, startling some members of his congregation, and causing the Rock to lose his place in his sermon. He stormed down, taking the steps two at a time. "Why don't you go back to Tarsus? Haven't you caused enough trouble already?"

He saw me, suddenly. He gave me a perfunctory kiss on the cheek, and went on, "Mother, why on earth are you consorting with this sort of riff-raff? This is one of our enemies.   When Stephen was stoned to death, he stood on the sidelines cheering! What insidious lies has he been telling you, to make you come all the way into the city?"

But while he was carrying on, some members of his flock seemed to have noticed that he called me mother, and they started to whisper among themselves — I could hear them — *Joshua's mother. Look, it's Miriam bat Joachim, the mother of the kvisatz haderach.* And presently one or two of them came closer, staring at me with curiosity — in some cases, animosity, for they knew Joshua had spoken ill of me sometimes, saying I misunderstood him, calling his followers his real family.

"Don't make a scene, James," I said. "Perhaps I didn't get duped into coming here by your turncoat Pharisee. Perhaps I merely wanted to see my children. I'm still your mother, you know, though you may think you've cut yourself loose, and sworn allegiance to this fanatical commune. I still want to make sure you're eating right."

"Yes, but to bring in *this* —" His glare was so venomous that most would have cowered, but Paul did not. Either he was extremely thick-skinned, or else the intensity of whatever it was he had experienced on his way to Damascus had made him impervious to contradiction. "Mother, you've no idea. This man's word has caused massacred a dozen innocents. He hates us. If you'd only seen Stephen when they stoned him —"

"James," I said, "I don't know why I agreed to come here with this man. His ideas are outlandish, and his grasp of the Torah is so muddled that even I was able to see holes in what he tried to tell me. But he's pushy, I'll give him that; he doesn't stop badgering; he'd wear down a mountain by talking at it. If he's sincere about changing sides, I think you should listen to him. I know he really thinks he saw something on that road; either he hit his head so hard when he fell off his horse that his wits have been permanently addled, or he encountered some luminous apparition of your brother that's changed him from within — or else he's just another salesman, promising a diamond inside every turd; who knows? All three, perhaps. But now, James, we should get ready for supper. The sun's going to set in an hour

or two, and your disciples here could use a little organizing. You were always messy, you boys, and moreover, it's Friday; it would be just like you not to be ready in time for sunset, and forced to eat a half-cooked supper on the Sabbath."
    ***

In the kitchen I encountered my old friend — my old nemesis too, in a manner of speaking — another Miriam, who had once been the most notorious whore in Nazareth, and whom my son had transformed into a veritable angel of goodness. We called her Magdala, for in a roomful of women it is possible to call out "Miriam" and have a dozen heads turn in response.

Miriam of Magdala had aged well. I had not. When she saw me, she threw the last batch of fish into the hot oil, and she hugged me fulsomely, her embrace smelling of anchovies and attar of roses.

"You still kohl your eyes," I said to her. I could not keep the envy out of my voice. She was still slender as a willow branch; she had not, of course, had seven children.

"And your tongue is still sharp," she said,

laughing. "Look at me! I've gone from courtesan to cook and cleaning woman. You've no idea how many mouths we feed here. The poor, the sick ... they have nowhere. It's a madhouse; it's always a race to get all the cooking done before sundown."

I did not really have to take charge, so I merely helped where I could; so did some other women, including two more Miriams. Though they all complained of the chaos and the disorganization, the truth was that they had the routine down quite well; there was, indeed, an order behind this seeming anarchy. By the time the shofar sounded, all the labor was done, and the women brought the food into the refectory, which was a large room filled with rude wooden tables and benches.

There was nothing Greek about this meal at all. This was strange, because sabbath meals, since Herod the Great's massive Hellenization of Judaea, have always tended to be a little Greek: perhaps a bit of flute music, a formal debate on the nature of love, an dance or a song. Not here. There were prayers in both Aramaic and in the Old Tongue. My son James and Joshua's old friend Simon Cephas led the chanting, the one in a reedy tenor, the other in a resonant bass. This was a throwback to a simpler, purer time, in keeping with the philosophy of the Essenes, which my son had received from John the Baptist.

Another son of mine, Jude, came up to me and kissed me diffidently on the cheek. I had not realized he was living with the group. Indeed, both my sons made much of me, and complimented me on the salt fish, though really it was largely Magdala's concoction.

"Yes, mother," James told me, "we really need you to get things going in the kitchen. No one came whip them into shape the way you can."

I missed them, I realized. I had been trying not to, and telling myself I was better off detached from all their nonsense, but I was surprisingly happy to see them.

Paul, to my surprise, sulked in a corner for the entire meal, and did not speak while the Rock gave a lengthy discourse on humility and patience, which seemed at times to be aimed directly at my traveling-companion. There were many pointed references to

Stephen, too; apparently they all believed Paul had connived in his death, which had alienated many of the Greek-speaking Jews and caused the community to shrink to a small group of locals.

But it was a good meal, prepared with love, and the sabbath guests — some of them poor people from off the street — were happy to be fed, and to hear that they too were worth something — the Rock made sure they understood that when he began his sermon with a string of beatitudes: blessed are the poor, the meek, and so on, all of which he attributed to my wayward firstborn. Most did not notice that Paul was being snubbed; most, I am sure, did not notice Paul at all, for all that he was fuming away in the corner.

At length, however, Paul asked leave to address the group; and since in this assembly everyone was allowed to speak from time to time, even prostitutes and lepers, he was accorded a brief, polite silence to begin his witnessing.

Paul began unconfidently, larding his Aramaic with two-shekel Greek words. He told the group he had been wrong about many things. He didn't admit to complicity in Stephen's death — not in so many words. But he *had* been a secret agent for the Sadducees.   He had written reports, made meticulous lists of blasphemies and unorthodoxies.   Not that he had personally had anyone stoned to death.   I could see that Paul was walking a fine line now, that he was perhaps glossing over certain realities that both he and the community knew about.   I had already caught him in one heinous inconsistency — he claimed to be the son of a strict rabbinical tradition — raised in silence no less! — and yet he also appeared to be a tentmaker.   Maybe the Jews in his native Tarsus didn't see any conflict between tanning hides and being a rabbi. After all, Paul didn't see a conflict between my being a virgin and having seven children.

On the other hand, hadn't Paul already given me his vision of truth and reality, and how the two need not be entirely congruent? I should have expected him to edit the facts a little, to shape them into a gripping, self-laudatory story.   But now he was getting to the heart of his argument ... his encounter with my son.

"He came to me out of the sky. He was clothed in light. He blinded me. He enfolded me in such warmth and radiance that I knew that I, unworthy, a miserable sinner, had stumbled into the arms of God."

This was when the disciples began snickering a little ... though they continued to listen politely. Magdala whispered in my ear, "If only he'd enfolded *me* when he was still alive, my dear; you of all people know how much I wanted him —" She really loved him still. One could forgive a lot, for the sake of so much love; I had long since come to terms with her notoriety. "The man's crazy."

Paul didn't seem to sense the unfriendly reaction. He went on talking. "Suddenly I realized that, even though his mission ended in unexpected death, even though the Roman Empire has not toppled, even though the great free Jewish nation has not miraculously been reestablished in the promised land, Joshua bar Joseph is still the kvisatz haderach. You were wrong to think of him as one of the many scrawny messiahs that even now sprinkle the countryside of Judaea and Galilee. He's a different kind of messiah. A messiah for the whole world. A messiah who takes the burden of our sins upon himself. A shining messiah who descended to earth so that we, touched by his infinite grace, would no longer be bound by the earth; a messiah who has built for us a highway to the bosom of God; *that's* the real Joshua bar Joseph — God didn't just direct his words and actions. God *was* his words and actions."

At that point, the laughter became open, and none too friendly. Oddly enough, only Magdala seemed to take him seriously — well, a little seriously at any rate — because she said to me, "There was something about that man that you couldn't pin down ... something otherworldly ... do you think ..."

"I suckled him," I said. "His appetite was human enough. My breasts did not start spewing forth ambrosia."

"I understand something else about him," said Miriam of Magdala, "something that perhaps you cannot see. He has a terrible need to be forgiven, this man. He torments himself daily over some terrible wrong he has done — and these wrongs are always far more terrible in the imagination than in fact — and he won't be happy until heaven and earth themselves declare that his sin has been washed away. I know what he's going through; I've gone through it myself."

Well, James and Jude stormed up to the dais where Paul had been speaking, and they forced him to sit down again. "I've heard enough," James said. "This is my brother you're talking about. We were close — well, we fought like cats and dogs, but I think that if Joshua was God, he'd probably have told me."

"That's right," said the Rock. "Joshua's never come down from the sky to visit any of us, and we were his best friends."

"But in Damascus they told me that many of you saw him in the flesh, after he rose from the dead —"

Jude said, "Joshua had four brothers. Some of us look a lot like him."

"But the empty tomb," Paul said. "There was an empty tomb. I heard the rumors." More laughter now. It was vicious laughter. My son would not have approved. Joshua never laughed at people.

"For years we've been trying to keep alive his hopes, his dream of purifying our Jewish faith," said James. "We've tried to live the lessons he taught us — sharing all our property, praying, trying to find the heart of the Torah instead of clinging to its surface. Soon the world as we know it will end. So now you come in with this pagan hocus-pocus. What's the use of it? The end times are already upon us — who can be bothered with a new religion now?"

"Joshua isn't just for Jews," Paul said, "and if there's a way of making him easier for the Gentiles to swallow —"

The laughter was raucous now, unbridled.

"You've been reading too many Greek philosophers," said Barnabas. "The Transcendence of the One, the Incarnation of Deity, I've heard effete young men babbling about such things in the wine-shops."

"Just how Greek are you, anyway?" James said. "Do you think Plato is the equal of Moses? Do you sneak pork sausages into your lodgings at night? Do you share them with some painted little boy?"

Instead of shrugging off this barrage of schoolyard Greek jokes, Paul rose to his feet and flung himself at James. He punched him in the solar plexus. He was a little man, but he must have been truly enraged, because my son actually staggered, clutched his stomach, toppled into a vat of stew. It was Cephas, a big man, and burly from reeling in nets all his life, who caught Paul in a headlock, and lifted him up, his bandy legs kicking at the air.

"I knew it!" Miriam of Magdala said to me. "Your friend's not too keen on the ladies. Oh, don't be shocked, mother; I can tell these things; I'm a professional, you know."

"You mean he practices abomination?"

"Really, Miriam!   I thought you were raised a little more modern than that.   I could be wrong anyway; maybe he's just shy."

"Stone him!" Jude shouted, and lobbed a hard roll at Paul's head, laughing. Another bread projectile clouted him in the cheek. Soon they were all doing it, jeering and cackling with all the exuberance of children ... they did not have death on their minds ... but they were killing him with ridicule.   In a crowning touch, a little boy — one of my grandsons — emptied a beaker of wine over

Paul's head.

Presently the Rock let Paul go, left him in a crumpled heap on the platform. The bread continued to fly for a few more moments, but presently there came a more sober moment, when another Miriam — she who owned the house — led the throng in a spirited rendition of a psalm — *As the hart pants for the waterbrooks, so longs my soul for thee, O God* — and I watched Paul trying to sit up, the breadcrumbs falling out of his hair. Paul listened to the singing. I could tell that he was bewildered by what had happened, alienated even; this little commune run by my sons and their friends possessed a sense of fellowship, of togetherness, while Paul was plagued by a perpetual not-belonging. My heart went out to him; it saddened me, yet I did not know what I could do.

"Mother," he said, coming to me, sitting at my feet, "help me."

"How can I?" I said. "Nobody believes you. I can't make them believe you, and I've already told you that I will not endorse your delusions. I think you should leave here, ride down to Caesarea, and take the first ship out back to Tarsus."

He broke the soggy loaf in his hand and absently chewed a piece. "I've got a lot of thinking to do," he said. "But I'm getting ideas. Even this hunk of bread is giving me ideas. Bread is life. You think you can smother this flesh and blood with bread and wine? I'll show these people, Miriam! Joshua will speak to me. He'll give me whatever weapons I need, whatever it takes to make a new covenant with the world." Amazing words for a little man who had just been pelted with buns. He drew himself up to his full height — what there was of it — and shouted: "All of you — I'm going away now. I'm going to commune with my redeemer, and when I come back, you won't be laughing anymore."

No one paid him any attention. He stormed out of the refectory and slammed the door, which occasioned some titters; there were no more disturbances that sabbath.

Paul left the city as soon as the sabbath ended and traveling was permitted again. Only Barnabas knew where he went; once when I asked him, he replied, vaguely, "Arabia." Perhaps, like the prophets he so wanted to be like, he had gone into the wilderness to commune with his peculiar god; though I think he loved comfort too much to remain in any wilderness for long. At any rate, I did not see him again for many years, and thought, indeed, that he would never come back.

A good thing came of it all; I visited with my children for some weeks; since I was already in Jerusalem, I stayed through Passover, worshiped at the Temple, and held my grandchildren in my arms, which reminded me a little of Shoshana, my little terracotta doll, buried by a rosebush, forty years before. I also renewed my ever-ambivalent friendship with Miriam of Magdala, who had so often been a surrogate daughter-in-law to me in the past, with all the good and the bad that that implies.

During Passover, I also saw Joseph of Arimathea, so frequently our family's benefactor, who seldom came to Jerusalem since my son's execution; and that put me in mind of our first meeting, forty years before.

2

If I skip lightly through the events sur-
rounding Joshua's birth, it is because it was
remarkably uneventful. As the years have
gone by, as Paul's uneasy hybrid of a religion
began snaking its way toward Rome,
Joshua's birth has acquired more and more
of the trappings of myth; not even Paul,
perhaps, had had any real inkling of the
public's hunger for miracles, or the credulity
of the converted.

When I was thirteen and pregnant, I had
never heard of Bethlehem. I knew nothing
of stables, stars, or wise men from the east.
If I gave birth in a cave, with only Ruth as
midwife in attendance, it was because my
husband wanted as little scandal as possible
to attend the birth; for from the wedding

until I was delivered of Joshua, barely seven months were to elapse. People talk. Even marriage cannot always prevent gossip, and *mamzer* is the most hateful of epithets, worse even than leper; I wanted no stigma for my child.

In the wake of Herod the Great's death, there had been a spate of messiahs, uprisings, and harsh military reprisals. Archelaus, who had seized the throne, had his father's savagery but neither his gift for organization nor his grand vision of a gleaming hellenized Judaea. In Galilee there were beheadings, flayings, crucifixions, and simple disappearances.

Indeed, many of my husband's colleagues had been summarily arrested by Archelaus's secret police and vanished without a trace. These were frightening times. People actually prayed for Rome to take direct control; for the Romans were at least predictable. The Carpenter, my husband, was a mild-mannered man, a learned man. He certainly harbored no enmity toward the regime, but some of his acquaintances had been known to espouse the doctrines of one kvisatz haderach or another; it was a matter of time before someone, under torture perhaps, would denounce him to the authorities.

That, and the imminent birth of my questionable child, were worrisome to us. I tried not to think of those things as I suckled my child in secret. Joseph indeed had named him, and thus established his legal claim to fatherhood; but there was a problem that would not go away; Joshua's eyes were the color of a cloudy sky over the Sea of Galilee; they were not the eyes of my husband. The Carpenter held me tenderly, hugged the baby, rocked him, kissed him, kissed me, professed great joy, and yet ... I knew he would always feel a little betrayed. And though he was too good a man to hound me about it, I knew he would always wonder about Joshua's father.

On the third or fourth day — I know it was before my son's circumcision ceremony — there came a messenger to the cave. I suppose, speaking Greek, Paul would have called him an angel.

It was one of those very deep caves, and the hill was almost half a day's walk from Nazareth and Sepphoris. Shepherds always know of such caves. There were rooms and passageways and twisty damp corridors; it seemed to me that though my child came forth into the world, we were still inside a kind of womb, a womb of earth and rock. Joshua's was an easy enough birth; Ruth knew midwifery well; had she not brought me into this world as well? But I was lonely. My mother came once, with a basket of loaves and fruit; Ruth watched over me, of course; my father did not come at all; the Carpenter, despite his protestations of love to me and my child, seemed not to want to spend much time with us.

I lay on my pallet, piled with as many soft blankets as could be found in the house, rocking my infant back and forth, looking into those eyes and remembering the alien embrace of the god, the heat of the flames, the smell of burnt corn and sizzling blood; I felt there were only the two of us, and the world had passed us by.

The angel came during one of Joseph's visits; later I realized that my husband had been followed. The Romans are efficient at detective work; there's nothing they won't find out, if they have a mind to it.

I heard him long before I saw him, for he came on horseback. The cave was lit entirely by torchlight, and when he rode into the cavern his shadow fell over me, long and wavering; Joshua stopped fretting all at once and started to giggle. When I looked up I saw that it was Pantera.

I had seen him naked, thought I would never see him again; this time he came to me in the burnished panoply of Rome. His breastplate, polished so that the torchlight danced about his features, was moulded to his musculature, and adorned in front with a relief of the gorgon, which is a dark, destructive aspect of their Great Mother. His cloak was finest Tyrrhian purple, and from his helmet sprouted a luxuriant red plume. He must have been in more battles since I last saw him. There was a new scar, one that traversed the old one on his left cheek and made a kind of "x" — that is a Greek letter, I am told, the initial letter of their world for messiah.

"Rejoice," he said — which is the Greek way of greeting a person — as he dismounted, a wooden box under his arm. "I have a few gifts, including one from the Senator himself; before he returned to Rome he asked me to give you this box, if the child lived."

As he walked toward me, he limped a little. There was a wound in his thigh, too; I saw the gash, unhealed, run from beneath his kilt all the way to his knee; he approached me slowly, with the box extended in both hands, as though it were an offering to the gods. And when he sat, in a dip in the stone floor, just in front of my pallet, he contrived to make it seem like an obeisance.

"The little girl," he said to my husband, "is now become a woman."

He gestured to Joseph that he should open the box, and the bitter fragrance of frankincense and myrrh filled the air when he did so, and I could hear the clink of coins.

"These are expensive gifts," said the Carpenter. "Didn't I turn down the thousand sesterces? You Romans always think there's a price for everything; my price, Pantera, is that you leave me at least the illusion of free will."

"It's a practical thing, Joseph," Pantera said. "You're going to need money, where you're going. Gold is the easiest to carry; it takes up less space; and the frankincense and myrrh is easily worth its weight in gold; there may be places along the way that won't take cash."

"Where am I going?" said Joseph.

I listened; it did not seem that I was being asked for my opinion. The baby began to fret again; modestly I turned away and held him to my breast; he murmured and began to feed, and I felt that profound communion that mothers and children feel at such moments; my mother would not have understood, since she had never suckled me.

Pantera did not answer Joseph directly, but merely explained, "There are lists. Lists with names on them. In Sepphoris, we have access to those lists. Do you understand?"

"Someone has proscribed me. Who?"

"Never you mind, Joseph. It seems you have made a few enemies. Did you ever espouse a prophet named Judas?"

"Everyone in Nazareth is named Judas," said Joseph, "except for the odd Joshua or two."

"There's a messiah in Galilee by that

name," said Pantera. "We've been hunting him down, We have him cornered somewhere in these hills. Your name was mentioned."

"Under torture, I suppose," my husband said grimly.

"Yes, yes," Pantera said. "You know the Roman law."

"That slaves cannot give evidence in a court of law unless they are first tortured? I've heard that law. Barbaric."

"Now don't be so high and mighty," Pantera said. "In your Jewish courts, a woman can't give evidence at all. Anyway, I'm here to help you, so stop arguing. The illusion of free will cuts both ways. Judaea is a client kingdom, not a province; Rome doesn't want to interfere in the minutiae ... so if your ethnarch chooses to stamp out a revolt with utter ruthlessness, and to make out lists of names and execute those persons just for the fun of it, Rome will just methodically round up those persons and crucify them. It's a matter of paperwork, of bureaucracy. But in your case ... there is the problem of the child."

"The child you have been bending over

backward to protect ... the little mamzer."

Hearing my husband say that word stung me, but I hugged my child closer to my bosom, and tried to wear the mask of the proper woman, who sees and hears nothing, and whose only thought is for the baking or the laundry.

"Yes," Pantera said, "the child of earth and starry heaven."

"What does that mean?" said Joseph.

"It's a phrase from the Mysteries," said Pantera, and would elucidate no further. "At any rate, we are rounding up messiahs, radicals, revolutionaries, subversives of every color. I know that you are probably innocent, but that's not the point; the massacre of innocents is a necessary evil; to maintain order, you have to have crucifixions. Nobody likes it, but terror is the best organizational tool we Romans have." He said all this by rote, as though he were repeating the instructions of some commanding officer. I know it disturbed him — he was, after all, from a subject race himself, and his Romanness came from a writ of citizenship, not from the heart. "But listen carefully. There are cracks in every wall.

We are going to let you slip away."

"Where are we going?" Joseph said.

"First, by military escort, to Caesarea," said Pantera, "and then, by ship, to Egypt. You are part of a cargo of olive oil. It was the best that could be arranged; the arrest warrant is already on the commander's desk, and he can only delay signing it so long."

"It seems so unfair!" Joseph said at last. "You know we've done nothing."

"Think of it as providence," Pantera said. "Think of it as a grand opportunity. You'll be a guest of Joseph of Arimathea, one of the richest men in Palestine, and you'll have the use of one of his houses in Egypt. You will be able to teach the Torah at one of the local synagogues, if you wish, and your eyes will be opened to the wider world — culture, Joseph! — philosophy, drama, science. And other ways of seeing even your own peculiar monotheism, and realizing that it's not some uniquely Jewish thing but has also been dreamt of within other systems of thought. Think of the advantages for your child, too, the wonders he'll see, the languages he'll be able to speak, Egyptian and Greek and Latin and Persian...."

"But these hills are our home," said my husband.

"Go quickly," said Pantera. "A maniple is waiting at the foot of the hill. Ride with the decurion to Nazareth, and pack as little as possible; you'll be provided for, and you can cash in part of the Senator's gift to buy new clothes once you reach Egypt. I'll stay here and guard your wife until you return."

The last sentence almost caused Joseph to lose his temper. For he had been peering at the baby, and at Pantera's eyes, and then at the baby again. He glared at the centurion, and seemed to be reaching for his dagger. But Pantera gripped my husband's wrist, and he said, softly, "We won't talk about what's in your mind. What's done was done by the god. It is written in the stars. We cannot undo it."

"You — you — my wife —"

"Don't say it," Pantera said.

And let go. And watched my husband as he left the cave, a sunken man, taking my bondswoman with him to help him pack, leaving me alone with the man he believed to have cuckolded him.

"I didn't mean to hurt him," Pantera said

softly. "The god used me. We won't speak of it either, you and I; what happened was between the earth and the sky; we were only bystanders."

I wept. "My husband hates me," I said. "He hates the baby. Why did you do those things to me? I was only a girl. I'm still only a girl. Your god destroyed my innocence."

"No, Miriam, no. You will never lose your innocence. May I hold the baby?"

He did not wait for my permission but stooped to pick Joshua from my arms. He bounced him a little gingerly on his knee. The baby spluttered a little and drooled on Pantera's shiny cuirass. The centurion's helmet caught the flickering torchlight and seemed to burn against the half-dark. It must have frightened Joshua, because he began to cry.

Pantera laughed. "A Homeric moment," he said. It was some Greek or Roman play on words, I supposed. He rocked my son back and forth until he quieted down, and looking at them I realized just how similar those eyes were, and I thought, God, God, were it not for those eyes, we would not be fleeing for our lives, and no one would dare call you a bastard....

3

At sea, I was as sick as could be. My first journey by water was appalling, and they have not improved with time. Only my baby never seemed out of sorts; I don't think he vomited even once.

By all accounts the trip from Caesarea to Alexandria was an easy one, and we traveled like royalty, for the captain gave us his own apartments. That in itself was strange, considering we left Judaea under a cloud of conspiracy, with a death-sentence hanging over my husband's head.

A Roman ship is the most wretched place on earth. Below decks, it is a veritable Sheol. The weeping and gnashing of teeth, of course, is unceasing, as is the rhythmic pounding of the hortator's drum, and the whine of the lead-tipped flagellum, and the groaning of tormented galley slaves.   The captain's quarters were not spacious, but they were at least private. My husband slept elsewhere.   He was still irritated, blamed this whole thing on me, I suspected, though in truth were it not for me he might already be dead.

At night, my baby in my arms, I dreamt of fire.   Perhaps it was the roar of the salt wind that reminded me of flames.   In the dream I was clutching my child and fleeing through a blazing city. Around us, temples and palaces were crumbling, aqueducts crashing, men and women with their arms spread wide on fire, like living, flaming crucifixes. I ran. I looked behind me for my husband, but he was not in this dream at all. I screamed out Joseph's name, but no one heard me. All were too wrapped up in their own misery. The sewage in the streets was aflame with a stench of death ... the streets were like rivers of fire.

I ran as Ionic columns snapped and statues of Roman gods tumbled and shattered. There were horsemen, too, with sickles, reaping the crowd.   There were flaming human heads flying through the sky like the stones from catapults.   Everyone was screaming. But my child was silent, gazing at the chaos with an eerie calm ... there was no fire reflected in his eyes ... only the profound gray sea. I ran.

At the center of the burning city there was a staircase ... my feet were bare, and the marble was cool, and the steps were lined with stone sphinxes, which are Egyptian cherubim; and the sphinxes sang, an otherworldly funeral music that keened above the hiss of flame and the screams of the dying ... and I started to ascend ... and as I climbed higher and higher, the marble became more and more translucent, until it seemed that it was not marble but glass, then not even glass but a sheer, incorporate substance, so that I was climbing stairs made of nothing at all ... and here the sphinxes lost their stony quality and became flesh, with mighty rushing wings and burning eyes, and I still I rose higher, until the burning city, no, the world, was far beneath me ...

And finally, at the summit, suffused with

starlight, there was a woman with many breasts, a woman like a mountain. The sun and the moon were her eyes, and when she opened her lips to speak, stars came cascading forth. And each of her breasts suckled a full grown man, and they were of all races and colors, including many strange types of men that I had never seen.

I gazed up at the woman in awe. The milk streamed from her many breasts and formed a river of stars across the sky.

"Who are you?" I whispered.

"A strange kind of a question," said the woman. "If you didn't already know, you would never have been able to find me."

I said, "I didn't expect to find you here ... I expected ... I don't know ... someone else."

"The One who has no Name, perhaps?"

She then uttered the Divine Name, which I had never heard uttered, and the heavens shook with laughter that was like the clanging of great bells. And the vault of heaven, which was like a shield of glass, cracked, and I saw in the jagged opening a light so fierce that I had to look away.

"What impertinence ... coming all the way up here to badger me with silly questions," said the woman. "I think I should ask you a thing or two. For example, what makes you think you can take my place? You suckle but a single infant — whereas, you can see, *I* sustain the whole world."

"I never claimed to replace you," I said. "I don't even know your name."

"Perhaps I too am Nameless," she said, and laughed again. "Or is Namelessness a monopoly of the males?"

Her laughter filled the sky. Below me, the city burned. Suddenly, my baby began to cry. I clasped him tightly to me. The city began to spin. The stars whirled and became streaks of light, and the laughter rang out, and all the sphinxes laughed, and as I quieted my son I realized that we were the still center of the wheeling cosmos, the focus, the heart; I and my son were the world.

The fire no longer pained me. It was a purifying fire. All that mattered to me was my child. Slowly the dream faded, and I founded myself once more in an alien bed, in a groaning ship, lurching through the humid night. Joshua was still, serene; I had been sure he was in the dream with me; his soul had not yet completely disentangled

itself from mine; we were still part of one
another.

Somewhere, a whipped slave howled.
I was afraid.

AUTHOR BIO
S.P. SOMTOW

The most well-known expatriate Thai in the world
—*International Herald Tribune*

Once referred to by the International Herald Tribune as "the most well-known expatriate Thai in the world," Somtow Sucharitkul is no longer an expatriate, since he has returned to Thailand after five decades of wandering the world. He is best known as an award winning novelist and a composer of operas.

Born in Bangkok, Somtow grew up in Europe and was educated at Eton and Cambridge. His first career was in music and in the 1970s he acquired a reputation as a revolutionary composer, the first to combine Thai and Western instruments in radical new sonorities. Conditions in the arts in the region at the time proved so traumatic for the young composer that he suffered a major burnout, emigrated to the United States, and reinvented himself as a novelist.

His earliest novels were in the science fiction field but he soon began to cross into other genres. In his 1984 novel Vampire Junction, he injected a new literary inventiveness into the horror genre, in the words of Robert Bloch, author of *Psycho*, "skillfully combining the styles of Stephen King, William Burroughs, and the author of the Revelation to John." *Vampire Junction* was voted one of the forty all-time greatest horror books by the Horror Writers' Association, joining established classics like *Frankenstein* and *Dracula*.

In the 1990s Somtow became increasingly identified as a uniquely Asian writer with novels such as the semi-autobiographical *Jasmine Nights*. He won the World Fantasy Award, the highest accolade given in the world of fantastic literature, for his novella *The Bird Catcher*. His seventy-seven books have sold about two million copies world-wide.

After becoming a Buddhist monk for a period in 2001, Somtow decided to refocus his attention on the country of his birth, founding Bangkok's first international opera company and returning to music, where he again reinvented himself, this time as a neo-Asian neo-Romantic composer. The Norwegian government commissioned his song cycle Songs Before Dawn for the 100th Anniversary of the Nobel Peace Prize, and he composed at the request of the government of Thailand his *Requiem: In Memoriam 9/11* which was dedicated to the victims of the 9/11 tragedy.

According to London's Opera magazine, "in just five years, Somtow has made Bangkok into the operatic hub of Southeast Asia." His operas on Thai themes, *Madana, Mae Naak,* and *Ayodhya,* have been well received by international critics. His opera, *The Silent Prince,* was premiered in 2010 in Houston, and, *Dan no Ura,* premiered in

Thailand in the 2013 season. Since then he has composed many more stage works including the acclaimed fantasy-based opera *The Snow Dragon* (premiered in Milwaukee in 2015) and seven operas in the *DasJati* sequence which aims to put all ten of the iconic *Ten Lives of the Buddha* into music drama form.

He is increasingly in demand as a conductor specializing in opera and in the late-romantic composers like Mahler. His repertoire runs the entire gamut from Monteverdi to Wagner. His work has been especially lauded for its stylistic authenticity and its lyricism. The orchestra he founded in Bangkok, the Siam Philharmonic, has mounted the first complete Mahler cycle in the region.

He was the first recipient of Thailand's "Distinguished Silpathorn" award, given for an artist who has made and continues to make a major impact on the region's culture, from Thailand's Ministry of Culture.

In 2017 he was awarded the European Cultural Achievement Award by the *Europa KulturForum,* citing his building of bridges between Asian and Western cultures.

BOOKS BY
S.P. SOMTOW

General Fiction
The Shattered Horse
Jasmine Nights
Forgetting Places
The Other City of Angels (aka Bluebeard's Castle)
The Stone Buddha's Tears
Miriam: Memoirs of a Goddess: Annunciation

Dark Fantasy
The Timmy Valentine Series:
  Vampire Junction
  Valentine
  Vanitas
Vampire Junction Special Edition
Moon Dance
Darker Angels
The Vampire's Beautiful Daughter

Science Fiction
Starship & Haiku
Mallworld
The Ultimate Mallworld
The Ultimate, Ultimate, Ultimate Mallworld
Beyond Mallworld

Chronicles of the High Inquest:
       Light on the Sound
       The Darkling Wind
The Throne of Madness
Utopia Hunters
Homeworld of the Heart
Chroniques de l'Inquisition - Volume 1 (omnibus)
Chroniques de l'Inquisition - Volume 2 (omnibus)
Inquestor Tales One: The Singing Moons
Inquestor Tales Two: A Woman Cloaked in Shadow
Inquestor Tales Three: The Child Collector
Inquestor Tales Four: The Space Between Spaces
Inquestor Tales Five: Goddess in the Ruins

The Aquiliad Series:
       Aquila in the New World
       Aquila and the Iron Horse
       Aquila and the Sphinx

Fantasy
The Riverrun Trilogy:
       Riverrun
       Armorica
       Yestern
The Riverrun Trilogy (omnibus)
The Fallen Country
Wizard's Apprentice
The Snow Dragon (omnibus)

Media Tie-in
The Alien Swordmaster
Symphony of Terror
The Crow - Temple of Night
Star Trek: Do Comets Dream?

Chapbooks
Fiddling for Waterbuffaloes
I Wake from a Dream of a Drowned Star City
A Lap Dance with the Lobster Lady
Compassion—Two Perspectives
The Bird Catcher
Another Avatar
Mallworld Becomes Elektra

Libretti
Mae Naak
Ayodhya
Madana
Dan no Ura
Helena Citronova
The Snow Dragon
Dasjati:
    Temiya - The Silent Prince
    Sama - The Faithful Son
    Bhuridat - The Dragon Lord
    Mahosadha - Architect of Dreams
    Nemiraj - Chariot of Heaven
    Prince Vessantara

Collections
My Cold Mad Father
Fire from the Wine Dark Sea
Chui Chai (Thai)
Nova (Thai)
The Pavilion of Frozen Women
Dragon's Fin Soup
Tagging the Moon
Face of Death (Thai)

Other Edens
S.P. Somtow's The Great Tales (Thai)
Terror Nova (in press)
Terror Antiqua (in press)
Alien Heresies
Other Avatars

Essays, Poetry and Miscellanies
Opus Fifty
A Certain Slant of "I" (in press)
Sonnets about Serial Killers
Opera East
Victory in Vienna (ed.)
Three Continents (ed.)
Nirvana Express
Caravaggio x 2
The Maestro's Noctuary
Nox: The Second Book of Dreams

AN APPEAL TO MY READERS

This publication was made possible because a few dozen people became my supporters by joining this website:

www.patreon.com/spsomtow.

I'm no longer doing these books with the backing of a vast New York publishing conglomerate. It's pretty much do-it-yourself, with all the labor-intensiveness, snatching time away from money-making activities, and sloppily trying to proofread one's own copy implies.

If a few dozen more people would sign up — or a few hundred — my ability to resume my science fiction career would be much enhanced. So, please consider it.

Supporters get to read all my books chapter by chapter — in their unenhanced, inaccurately proofred and yet-to-be refined incarnations — right as they come out of my head. They get Christmas presents (though I am habitually late with them). You can join for as little a $2 a month — or as much as you'd like!